The Great Meow Mystery

Dandi Daley Mackall
Illustrated by Kay Salem

CPH.
SAINT LOUIS

To my sister Maureen—
in memory
of all our great childhood adventures
and all our great pets.

Copyright © 1997 Dandi Daley Mackall
Published by Concordia Publishing House
3558 S. Jefferson Avenue, St. Louis, MO 63118-3968
Manufactured in the United States of America

All rights reserved. No part of this publication may be reproduced, stored in a retrieval system, or transmitted, in any form or by any means, electronic, mechanical, photocopying, recording, or otherwise, without the prior written permission of Concordia Publishing House.

1 2 3 4 5 6 7 8 9 10   06 05 04 03 02 01 00 99 98 97

Cinnamon Lake Mysteries

*I'm not sure how we got famous
as the Cinnamon Lake Mystery Club.
I mean, the Cinnamon Lake part
is easy. That's where we live.
The mystery part is more ...
mysterious.*

Contents

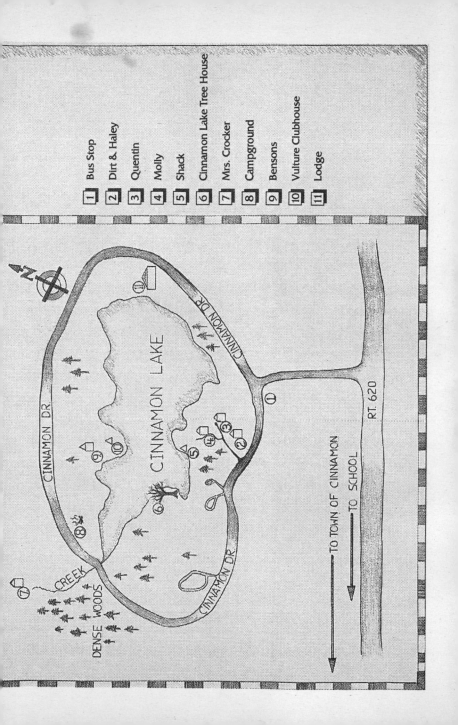

1 Bus Stop
2 Dirt & Haley
3 Quentin
4 Molly
5 Shack
6 Cinnamon Lake Tree House
7 Mrs. Crocker
8 Campground
9 Bensons
10 Vulture Clubhouse
11 Lodge

CINNAMON LAKE

CINNAMON DR.

CINNAMON DR.

CINNAMON DR.

CREEK

DENSE WOODS

RT. 620

TO TOWN OF CINNAMON

TO SCHOOL

1

Read All about It!

"Extra! Extra! Read all about it!

"Two-Headed Birth in Cinnamon Lake!

"Mystery Killing Uncovered by Vultures!

"Near-Death Experience on Cinnamon Drive!

"Read all about it!"

The shouts reached me on the lane before I could see the school bus stop. I didn't have to see who was yelling. Sam Benson!

"Molly! Molly! No fair!" Haley met me with her usual whine. Fallen leaves swirled around her feet. But her dark hair was perfect as always.

"Did you hear what the Vultures did?" she cried. "Sam and Ben Benson and Marty have started their own newspaper! Now nobody will buy our *Cinnamon Lake News*! No fair!"

Putting out our own newspaper was supposed to earn us enough money to build a real tree house. So far our Cinnamon Lake Club tree house was just tree—no house.

The Vultures already had a great club house across the lake from our tree. But they would do anything to wreck our plans. Like starting up a paper to put ours out of business. "Haley—"

Before I could say anything, Sam started yelling again. "Get your copy of the *VIP, Very Important Paper,* right here! Only a quarter!"

A quarter! Ours was a dime. But all around, kids were reading the *VIP.* The rack of *Cinnamon Lake News* was full. Sam waved his paper. It even looked like a newspaper. I ran ours off on my mom's copy machine.

"Where's Quentin?" I asked.

Haley pointed. "There he is—the traitor!"

Quentin is one of us. But he was standing on tiptoes, reading the back of a tall kid's *VIP.* I threw a handful of leaves at him.

"Molly!" he scolded. He's only in third grade like me. But he thinks he's grown up.

"Well, stop reading the enemy's paper!" I scolded back. "Don't you want them to buy ours?"

Quentin's thick glasses made his eyes look huge. "Is it my fault the youth of Cinnamon Lake prefer the *VIP?* Don't ask me why every eye is not glued to our headlines. Let us see …"

Quentin pulled a *Cinnamon Lake News* off the wooden rack. He started with my headline: "*Mums in Bloom* by Molly Mack. If that isn't exciting enough, there's *Geese Fly South* by Haley Harrison. Or my own *New Neighbor Moves In*. Or, turn to Dirt's cartoon of who-knows-what."

Dirt is the youngest member of our Cinnamon Lake club. I wasn't sure, but I thought her picture was of the Dumpster. Okay. So our paper wasn't doing well. Quentin didn't have to rub it in.

"At least we don't make stuff up like the Vultures," I said.

"Indeed," Quentin answered. "Who would make up a story about flowers growing?"

Sam's voice rang out, *"Mystery Killing Uncovered!"*

"What's that about?" I asked.

Quentin sighed. "I uncovered bird bones in my backyard. My cousin Martin thinks a cat

8

did it. He stole my news. Called it a mystery killing."

"Yeah," Haley agreed. "Like that *Two-Headed Birth* article. All it really said was that Mrs. Kelly had twins. And I wasted a quarter!"

"Way to go, Haley," I said.

Mr. Winkle, our bus driver, pulled in and screeched to a stop. Ben Benson, in true Vulture style, shoved in front of Quentin. Even chubby Quentin is no match for Ben. Ben and Marty look like they should be in high school instead of fifth grade.

Sam Benson pushed between Quentin and me. "It's a shame we're all sold out," he said. "Now you'll never know about the near death on Cinnamon."

Sam, Ben's brother, is in third grade too. But he's a Vulture all the way. Sam ran his fingers through his shiny, red hair. I ran my fingers through my own blonde hair. Compared to Sam's, my hair is dull straw. And Sam's eyelashes are twice as long as mine. As Haley would say, *Unfair!*

"Not interested, Sam," I said. I climbed the bus steps, said hello to Mr. Winkle, and sat in the first empty seat. Haley made me scoot over. Sam slid into the seat behind us.

"It's all about how Ben almost ran over a garter snake on his bike," Sam explained. He flashed his perfect smile at me.

"A garter snake on a bike?" I asked.

"No, Molly," Sam said. "Just buy the paper for yourself. Oops. Forgot. They're all sold out."

I looked around the bus at all the VIPs. Nobody was reading the Cinnamon Lake News. Quentin sat in front. Haley was next to me. Only Dirt was missing.

"Haley," I said. "Where's Dirt? We need to talk about our newspaper."

"Not Dirt," Haley said.

"Why not?" Dirt, Haley's little sister, is the toughest first-grader in the world. She's 100 times tougher than Haley.

"Didn't you hear?" Haley said. "I thought you'd know by now, Miss Molly the News-woman."

"Heard what, Haley?"

"Chicken pox. Ugly, red spots from her head to her toes. And she can't leave her room."

"Poor Dirt!" I said. I thought about when I had chicken pox. Mom made me wear gloves so I wouldn't scratch myself to pieces.

"Poor Dirt, nothing!" Haley whined. "Poor *me*. *I* had chicken pox in the summer. *I* didn't even get to miss school."

"Quentin?" He was still trying to read the *VIP* over a kid's shoulder. "Are you in on this or what?"

"What?"

"We have to come up with a super story. Better than the *VIP*. Dirt has chicken pox and—"

"I can see the *Cinnamon Lake* front page now," Quentin said. He was using his smart aleck voice. "*Dirt Has Chicken Pox*. That should sell a few papers."

"If you let me finish," I said. "I was going to say that Dirt has chicken pox. So it's up to us to save our paper."

I stared out the bus window and thought about our morning paper. I watched as we passed three Amish farms. Dark blue clothes in all different sizes hung on a clothesline and flapped in the breeze. In one field, two teams of workhorses marched in straight rows.

"We could start with more interesting headlines," I said as we bumped onto Route 620. "Of course, we won't lie. Just tell the truth in a more interesting way. Like, instead of saying the mums were blooming, say *Giant Plants Push through Earth's Crust!*"

Quentin narrowed his brown eyes. "I suppose you expect me to write *Invader Moves In* instead of *New Neighbor*."

"Molly?" Ashley Taylor put her hand on my shoulder. Tall, blonde, and beautiful, she looks like *she* should be Haley's sister instead of Dirt.

"Me?" I asked. At school, Ashley's too popular to talk to me.

"Do you see any other Mollies?" she asked. "I want to know if you've seen Fluffy, my cat?"

"No," I answered. Back to Quentin. "What we need, Quentin, is a story so big, Ben Benson will be crying to read it."

"Because my dad said Fluffy didn't show up last night or this morning," Ashley said. "I just thought since you're part of Cinnamon Lake too—"

"No, Ashley," I said. "Sorry."

12

"Perhaps Fluffy has finally stood up for himself," Quentin said. "I told you to stop putting dresses on him."

"Some Cinnamon Lake Mystery Club," Ashley said as the bus pulled into the town of Cinnamon. "It's a mystery you're a club at all!"

Back to business. Where was I going to find a really great story?

Kyle Johnson, across the bus aisle, kept clearing his throat. He's in first grade, like Dirt. Kyle usually sits as far away from Dirt as possible. I like him. He reminds me of my little brother, Chuckie.

"You okay, Kyle?" I asked him.

"I just wondered if Ashley's cat could be with Big Shot, my kitty," Kyle said.

"Why?" Quentin asked. "Did you dress Big Shot up too?"

"No!" Kyle said.

My nose for news started itching. "Kyle?" I asked. "What about your cat?"

"Big Shot is missing too," he said.

I reached across the aisle and slapped my hand over Kyle's mouth. "Don't say another word," I whispered.

Kyle's eyes got big. He nodded up and down.

I sank back in my bus seat, leaned into Haley, and motioned for Quentin. "I've got it!" I whispered.

"Talk in meaningful sentences, Molly," Quentin said. "You have what?"

"Our story," I said. "One everybody in Cinnamon Lake will buy. Tree house, here we come!"

"What are you talking about?" Quentin asked.

"I'll tell you what I'm talking about. The Great Cinnamon Lake Meow Mystery!"

2

Divided We Fall

After school I got my bike and raced to the Cinnamon Lake tree house. The breeze felt like a stream of cold water on my face. The roads were paved with leaves that crunched under my bike tires.

As usual, I was the first one there. The only Cinnamon Lake member who could beat me was Dirt. And she was home with chicken pox.

I leaned my bike against a tree and walked down the hill to our clubhouse. Even though we don't have a tree *house*, it's a great tree.

I climbed to my branch, the highest. From there, Cinnamon Lake seemed framed with orange and red. Trees lined the shore. I thanked God for coming up with colors.

I don't know why Dirt and Haley and Quentin made me president of the Cinnamon Lakers. Sometimes I think Quentin feels *he* should be the leader. Maybe that's why I wanted so much for our newspaper to work out. And I was tired of the Vultures wrecking our plans.

Down below, I heard leaves stirring. "Rabbit food," Quentin mumbled as he came down the hill. "A man puts in a long, hard day. What does he get? Food fit for long-eared beasts." He chomped on his carrot.

I figured Quentin's mom had him on another diet. "Come on up, Quentin!" I hollered.

"If I have the energy," he said. "Did your mother send treats?"

"Nope," I said. "Sorry." Quentin loves my mom's cookies, especially when *his* mom puts him on a diet.

"No fair!" Haley's voice reached us before she did. She was picking her way down the hill. "Mother made brownies for Dirt," Haley whined. "And all I get is this one, tiny, left-over brownie."

Quentin stopped climbing. "Did she say *brownies*?" His voice cracked on the word.

Haley wiped crumbs from her mouth. She still wore a pink dress so climbing wasn't easy, even though her branch is the lowest. Quentin moaned at lost brownies and settled onto his branch.

I called the meeting to order. The sunlight coming through the fall leaves dotted our faces with reddish light.

"We're here to talk about making our newspaper Number 1 in Cinnamon Lake!" I said, trying to get them stirred up.

"Nobody buys our papers," Haley griped. "They buy the *VIP*."

"That's about to change," I told her. "Our next paper will *make* them buy it."

"How?" Haley asked.

"The Great Cinnamon Lake Meow Mystery!" I shouted.

Quentin groaned.

"What's a meow mystery?" Haley asked. But she seemed more interested in her chipped fingernail polish than in the story of the decade.

"Ashley's cat, Fluffy, and Kyle's cat, Big Shot, are missing," I said.

"So what?" Haley asked.

"As much as it hurts me to do so, I must agree with Haley," Quentin said. "The cats will turn up. If they have adventures, they are not likely to tell us."

Quentin may be the smartest kid I know, but he has no imagination. "Quentin," I said, trying to stay calm, "we'll make our news and sell our papers *before* the cats turn up. Get it?"

Quentin raised an eyebrow. "This does not compute, Molly," he said.

The breeze carried a shower of leaves. "I don't get it either," Haley said, brushing a leaf off her pink dress.

Where was Dirt when I needed her?! "We sell it as a big mystery," I explained. "Can't you see it? *Cats Disappear from Cinnamon Lake! Cat Owners in a Panic!* That should at least sell as many as *Near Death on Cinnamon Drive!*"

"Then what?" Haley asked, sounding a *little* bit interested.

"Then we solve the mystery!" I said. "We find the cats and write the story before the Vultures know what hit them!"

Quentin squirmed on his branch. "Just because you found Dirt that time she was missing—it doesn't mean you can find missing cats. Even if they *were* missing. We are *not* detectives, Molly," he said.

I hate it when Quentin talks to me like I'm a child. "We don't have to be detectives, Quentin," I said. "We'll just be good reporters. Like Mr. Adams taught us."

Mr. Adams is our third-grade teacher. He did a whole unit on newspapers. "We'll answer the five *W*'s," I said. "Who, What, When, Where, and Why."

"As I tried to explain to Mr. Adams," Quentin said, shaking his head, "*why* should come first. It alone is the all-important question." Quentin started climbing down.

"Wait!" I yelled. "The meeting isn't over."

"It is over for me," Quentin said, dropping to the ground. "Science calls. Mother's taking me to the library on her way to the allergy doctor."

"No fair!" Haley said. "Just because you hate cats!"

I didn't think it was fair either. "But what about Big Shot and Fluffy?" I shouted after him.

Quentin still had his back to us. "Leave them alone and they'll come home, wagging their tails behind them," he said in a hoarse singsong.

"Quentin!" I hollered after him. "Our paper!"

But he pretended he didn't hear me.

I took a few deep breaths. Quentin knew just how to make me crazy! "Come on, Haley," I said. "We'll do it without Mr. Science."

I hopped down and waited for her. She made sure every inch of her pink dress stayed in place as she climbed to the ground.

"We'll go see Dirt," I said. "She'll help us."

"Did you forget already?" Haley asked. She stepped to the ground. "Dirt has chicken pox. She has to stay in her room."

"She could at least help us figure out the mystery," I said.

"Mother made me promise not to ask Dirt to do anything. Little Princess Dirt is supposed to rest."

I had to look away so I wouldn't laugh. Haley is the only *princess* in that house. Dirt would probably slug you if you called her that. We walked without talking. The only noise came from geese honking signals to each other.

I was thinking about Quentin. I couldn't believe he left us like that. Didn't he want to beat the Vultures in the newspaper game? What kind of Cinnamon Laker was he anyway? And worst of all, how was I going to solve the Cinnamon Lake Meow Mystery with nobody to help but Haley?

3

Cool, Colorful Dirt

Haley opened the door to her house and ran up the stairs. I followed, but Mrs. Harrison stuck out her arm and stopped me.

"Whoa!" she said. Mrs. H. was dressed in yellow leotards. She was in one of her skinny times. It seemed like only last week she was very plump. Sam says Mrs. H. has lost and gained and lost enough weight to make up a whole other mom.

"Molly … *puff … puff.* What can I … *puff … puff …* do for you?" She jogged in place as she barred me from entering. I heard the TV leader in the background. "Bend those knees!"

"I want to visit Dirt. Is she okay?" I asked.

"Have you … *puff …* had chicken pox?" she asked.

I promised I had.

The music from the living room stopped. So did Mrs. H. "Whew! Okay. But don't tell her anything to upset her. We're having enough trouble keeping her in her room."

Haley appeared on the stairs. "You can't tell Dirt about the c-a-t-s," she said.

"C-a-t-s?" Mrs. H. repeated. "Whatever it is, don't tell Dirt if it will make her want to escape—I mean, leave her room."

I was disappointed. If I couldn't get Quentin in on the mystery, I really needed Dirt. But I understood. If Dirt got into the cat mystery, nothing could keep her in her room. "Okay," I said.

Outside Dirt's closed door, I took a deep breath. I figured it might be the last fresh air I'd get for a while. I could only imagine what Dirt's room would look like after two days of Dirt trapped inside. I knocked.

"Yeah? Come in."

Easier said than done. I had to push my shoulder to the door. Bats, balls, clothes, and books pushed back.

"Dirt?" I asked, ducking a mop handle attack.

Dirt was across the room on her bed. Between her and me was a garbage dump. Wads of paper made an ocean of white on the floor.

I took one step. My foot rolled. Crayons. I spotted dozens of broken crayons under the paper wads. Paint brushes. Markers. Little empty plastic food coloring bottles.

Carefully, I made my way to Dirt. All day Haley had stayed wrinkle-free. Like tinfoil when you tear it off the roll. Dirt looked rumpled. Like foil after you wad it into a ball.

Dirt sat hunched over a notebook. She scribbled fast with a black crayon. I tried to get a look at what she was writing. Every inch of paper was covered with a different color.

"Dirt, what are you doing?" I tried to clear a place on the bed to sit.

"Something," Dirt said.

She stopped long enough to scratch the back of her hand. What Haley said was true. Dirt had spots on her hands, her feet, her face. Head to toe!

I waved my hand at the piles of paper wads. "What's all this, Dirt?"

Haley stuck her head in the door. "My weird sister thinks she's going to invent a

brand-new color. Isn't that the dumbest thing you ever heard? Ask her what she's going to name her dumb old color!"

"If I wanted a *dumb* color," Dirt said, "I'd name it *Haley*. But since it will be the best color in the world, I'm calling it *dirt*."

"Told you it was dumb," Haley said.

Dirt gave her sister her best *dirt* look. Haley left.

I sat in silence with Dirt for a while. She covered part of a page with green. Then she colored over the green with red. Frowning, she studied the paper, growled. Then she wadded it up and added it to the pile on the floor.

She started over. This time, Dirt sprinkled drops of blue food coloring on a piece of white cloth. Then she threw the empty bottle across the floor. She dropped red food coloring over the blue. The colors spread slowly into every corner of the cloth until none of it was white.

Once Dirt muttered, "Almost! Just about had it that time."

I looked, but couldn't tell any difference from all the other scribbles. A trail of dried leaves led from the bed to the window. I had a feeling Mrs. H. was right. Dirt had been escaping.

"Well," I said, after watching Dirt for awhile. "I'd better get home for supper. Still have a newspaper to get out."

"How did my tractor picture come out?" she asked.

Tractor picture? So it wasn't a Dumpster. "Great!" I said. "Don't worry about doing one for tomorrow though. We're doing a special edition."

"What?" Dirt stopped her coloring.

Rats. I'd promised not to say anything about the missing c-a-t-s.

"I mean, we're running pretty late. I won't have much time to type it."

Dirt shrugged and went back to coloring. "Man! What I need is something fuzzy to try out my new color on. Imagine dirt-colored dogs. Far out."

I left Dirt's room, trying to miss the mine field of deadly crayons.

That night Haley came over to work on the newspaper. After a couple of hours, we felt pretty proud of ourselves. Even Quentin's gray cells couldn't have done better. That's what he calls thinking—using his gray cells.

True, we didn't have much in the way of stories. But our headlines were going to give the *VIP* a run for its money!

4

A Couple of *W*'s

Missing Cat Mystery

Cats Disappear from Cinnamon Lake

Cat Owners Scared

Our headlines! The *Cinnamon Lake News* was the hottest thing going that cold, frosty morning at the bus stop.

Only two kids bought the *VIP*. Their best headline was "Vampires in Haunted House." The truth was Mrs. Crocker had a baby bat in her chimney.

I kept telling myself our headlines were nothing but truth—told in an interesting way.

If cat owners weren't actually scared yet, they would be.

Sam ran up and grabbed a paper without paying. "So the Cinnamon Lakers are actually selling papers," he said. "Now that *is* news."

Sam left, and Haley whispered, "If Big Shot and Fluffy can just stay away one more night, we can make a lot of money."

"Wait till Quentin sees what we did without him," I said. "Now he'll want in on the cat caper."

"Excuse me," Quentin said, pushing between us.

I hadn't seen him come up. He didn't even look at the paper!

Quentin marched to the bus line, his nose in a book. I couldn't believe it! This was the first time we'd sold newspapers to anybody except our parents! You'd at least think Quentin could say "Good job!"

"Well, Haley," I said loud enough for Quentin to hear. "With Dirt and *Quentin* out of the picture, it's up to us. We'll have to find those missing cats all by ourselves."

Quentin didn't ride the bus home. So Haley and I began the five *W*'s without him.

"How do we know which *W* to start with?" Haley whined.

I knew Quentin thought you should start with *Why*. But we needed some answers quick. Before the cats turned up on their own. *Why* somebody might steal cats was too hard. That left us who, what, when, and where.

"Let's start with *Where* and *When*," I suggested. "We can answer those by interviewing the owners of the lost cats. That should give us enough for another newspaper. Or at least another day's worth of headlines."

We started toward Ashley's dad's cabin. When her parents were still together, they had only used the cabin on weekends or holidays. Now Mr. Taylor lived there year round.

I had to pull Haley with me up to the door of Mr. Taylor's cabin. After a few knocks, the door opened wide.

"Hi, girls," Mr. Taylor said. "Magazine sales already?"

"No, sir," I said. "We've come about your cat. Fluffy?"

"Oh, did you find him?" Mr. Taylor looked behind us.

I felt bad for getting his hopes up. "No. We're reporting on the missing cat story," I explained.

I pulled out my reporting notebook. At the top of the first page, I wrote *When?*

"Mr. Taylor," I asked. "When did you last see Fluffy?"

Mr. Taylor wrinkled his forehead. "I'm not sure. Tuesday morning? Yes, I saw Fluffy in the morning. I sure hope he turns up soon. It's not like him to run off. Ashley will be very unhappy if Fluffy doesn't come back."

I scribbled: *Last seen Tuesday morning.* "And *where* was Fluffy when you last saw him?"

"In my backyard," he answered.

I wrote *"Taylor's backyard"* on the next page, below *Where.*

Mr. Taylor smiled at Haley. "Don't you have any questions for me ... Haley, isn't it?"

"Yes," Haley said. "I'd like to know if Ashley gets permanents. 'Cause she says her hair is naturally curly."

"Haley!" I said.

Mr. Taylor laughed.

"Well, thanks for your time," I told him. "We'll let you know when we find your cat."

"How could you ask Mr. Taylor that?" I said, once we were out of his yard.

"Like *your* questions were so great?" Haley said. "Fluffy has been gone since Tuesday. So what? I'll bet Ashley stole her own cat just to get attention. She always has to be the center of attention."

Kyle was sitting in a pile of brown leaves when Haley and I walked up. He wiped at his red eyes. "Ben Benson said Big Shot was taken by the dog food people. Is it true? Did they turn Big Shot into dog food?"

"No way!" I said. "That's just the Vulture's idea of a joke, Kyle."

"But your paper said cat owners are all scared it will happen to their cats." Kyle's sad eyes gazed up at me.

"Yeah," I said, feeling something like a pin-prick inside. "But that was just newspaper talk, Kyle. We'll find Big Shot."

It didn't take much to get Kyle to answer the two *W*'s. Big Shot disappeared from Kyle's yard on Tuesday.

Haley and I walked back toward her house. "Can we make up good enough head-lines with only two *W*'s?" Haley asked.

"I don't think so," I said. "We need another *W*. Like ... *what? * What really happened to those cats?"

I wasn't too worried about Big Shot and Fluffy. My biggest worry was that the cats would turn up before we got another bestselling *Cinnamon Lake News* out of the deal.

But all that was about to change.

"Isn't that Nicole?" Haley asked.

Nicole Blake came running right at us. A first-grader, she only comes up to my shoulders. She hung on my arm and tried to catch her breath.

"Nicole!" I said, patting her curly hair. "What's wrong?"

"It's Tiger!" she said, panting. "My ... kitty! Fluffy and Big Shot aren't the only disappeared cats. Tiger's gone too!"

5

The Third *W*

"You can count me out, Molly Mack!" Haley said, when we reached her house. She folded her arms in front of her. "I refuse to go out in the dark and look for cats! Not now!"

"But Haley—" I tried.

"No! Before, I thought Fluffy and Big Shot were just lost. But three lost cats? I don't think so! Somebody probably really did steal them! I don't want any part of that."

"How am I going to answer the third *W* all by myself?" I begged.

But Haley turned her back and walked into her house.

The sun was starting to set. I looked up and down the road. Nobody was outside. I felt a shiver run down my spine. I don't think I ever felt more alone. First Dirt. Then

Quentin. Now Haley. All had left me to carry on alone.

What was going on with the cat population in Cinnamon Lake? The cat mystery story was turning out to be more than a story. For the first time I felt scared. "I'm alone and frightened," I whispered to Jesus. "Please help me know what to do."

At home, Mom was still waiting for Dad. But she let me and my little brother, Chuckie, go ahead and eat. Spaghetti. I gulped mine down. Chuckie washed his face in his. He doesn't believe in silverware.

I thought about how much Quentin loves spaghetti. I missed Quentin. This was no time for pride. My prayer helped me decide that. I decided I'd swallow my pride and go see Quentin. If anybody could help me, he could.

As soon as I finished dinner, I headed for Quentin's. I was racing out the door when Chuckie caught me.

"Chuckie come?" he asked, giving me his sad puppy look.

"No," I said. "Chuckie stay."

"Peese, Mowy?" (Which means *Please, Molly?*) "Chuckie berry good."

Chuckie is almost never berry good.

Mom appeared with a dish towel in her hand. "That's nice, Molly." She gave Chuckie's face a swipe. "Take your brother."

"Mom!" I complained.

"And don't stay out late," she added quickly.

It was no use arguing. I walked fast to Quentin's, not saying a word to Chuckie. I wondered what it would be like to be an only child, like Quentin.

Chuckie trailed behind. "Wait for me, Mowy!" he called.

A woodpecker tapped in the distance. Leaves blew in circles, as if God were stirring them.

Quentin was standing in his driveway. In his hand was a large, brown bag.

"Whatcha got?" I hollered.

He stuck the sack behind his back. Quentin stared at Chuckie. Then at me. "Spaghetti?" he asked. He licked his lips. "Mother served codfish and sprouts. She's into vitamins this month. Especially vowels. A and E."

He shuffled backwards, toward his garage. The sack, he kept hidden behind his back.

I followed him. Chuckie followed me. The

neighbor's calico cat, Callie, ran out and brushed against my leg.

"Here, boy," Chuckie called.

"Calico cats are always females," Quentin informed my brother.

"Hi, girl," I said. I reached down to pat Callie. "Quentin, another cat is missing. Tiger. Haley and I interviewed Kyle and Mr. Taylor. We answered two of the *W* questions, *when* and *where* the cats disappeared. But we need help. One more *W* at least."

"Yeow!" Callie cried. Chuckie had tried to pet her. He'd ended up pulling her tail. Callie dove under a bush. Suddenly, the cat darted back and charged Quentin.

"Why does she want you?" I asked. "I thought you didn't like cats, Quentin."

"Shoo!" Quentin tried to keep Callie away with his toe. But she began climbing up his leg. She wanted that bag!

"Quentin, what do you have in that bag?" I asked.

Quentin had to hold the sack over his head to keep it from Callie. "Oh, all right," he said.

He held out his brown bag, shook it. Then slowly he opened it.

I peeked in. The smell almost knocked me

over. "Gross!"

Chuckie ran up to look. He scrunched his face and held his nose. "Kint stink!" he cried.

That's the way Chuckie says *Quentin*. I tried not to laugh. "What is it, Quentin?"

"Fish plus catnip." Quentin pushed each word through his closed teeth.

"Why do you have fish and catnip? I don't get it, Quentin."

"I ... I ... I wanted to find the wandering cats," he said. "That is what I'm doing. You want to answer the reporter question, *What?* That is precisely the purpose of this bag."

"Huh?" I muttered. For the smartest kid in class, Quentin wasn't making much sense.

"*What* happened to the cats?" Quentin said. "We pull my wagon full of catnip and fish all over Cinnamon Lake. The lost cats will come running. And that will be the end of that. Mystery solved. Case closed."

To tell the truth, I wasn't sure I wanted to end the mystery. At least, not until we sold another day's worth of newspapers. "I guess we can still get a good story for tomorrow's paper," I said. "Tell it in an interesting way. Three *W*'s would be news."

Quentin sighed. "Wait here."

When he returned, he was pulling his old wagon.

"Me ride!" Chuckie screamed when he saw it.

"You not ride," Quentin said.

He handed me the bag. I opened it, held my breath this time, and reached in. The squishy, slimy stuff made me shiver. Out came catnip balls. Catnip in gray cloth, shaped like a mouse. Socks filled with catnip. I left the fish in the bottom of the bag.

We taped catnip all over Quentin's wagon. Chuckie helped. Sort of. Last, we made a string of catnip balls for a wagon tail.

All the while, Callie Cat scratched at us. She purred and rubbed against the wagon. Then she pawed the catnip.

"Let's just dump the fish in the wagon," Quentin said.

"Good idea," I said. But when he did it, I gagged.

"Chuckie ride!" said my brother. Before I could stop him, Chuckie jumped right into the middle of fish and catnip.

"Oh, Chuckie!" I cried.

He grinned. "Giddyup, Kint!"

6

Cat Parade

Quentin shook his head at Chuckie, who was covered with raw fish. The wagon bumped down the rocky driveway. Callie chased at the tail of catnip. Chuckie squealed.

At the end of the lane, Quentin stopped short.

"Go!" Chuckie screamed. He held to the sides of the wagon and kicked. *Bang! Bang! Bang!*

Quentin didn't move. He didn't look me in the eyes either. "Um, Molly? Why don't *you* pull the wagon? I ... er ... I shall gather the cat owners. They should be present to identify their missing cats."

I knew what was going on. Quentin was chickening out. He probably felt silly pulling a smelly wagon. Where was Dirt when you needed her! She would have loved pulling the wagon. Smelly fish and all.

Chuckie was still yelling giddyup. I sighed and took the wagon handle. Quentin turned and headed for his house.

The wagon clanked and rattled as I bumped onto a gravel road. Callie stuck right with Chuckie and me. She was meowing like I'd never heard before! If those missing cats didn't hear or smell us, they were long gone!

I felt I was on a mission. Molly Mack, ace reporter. Molly Mack, ace detective. I imagined the scene: People lining the streets. I show up with the missing cats. Kids rush out and shake my hand. Grown-ups clap and cheer. I'd be the hero in our own headline!

"Kitty!" Chuckie's squeal broke into my dream.

I turned to see two cats running full speed to the wagon. A black and white cat batted at the wagon's catnip tail. Another one tried to jump in with Chuckie. The cats hissed at each other. They let out low cat growls.

I pulled the wagon in the pitch darkness of a cloudy sky. Each time we came to a lighted house, I checked my cargo. I knew cats were there, fighting each other for the smelly treats. But it wasn't until I pulled into a clearing that I could get a good look by the light of a front porch.

I couldn't believe my eyes! Quentin's plan was working! Six cats formed a parade behind me.

I led the crying cats to Cinnamon Drive. Several people came off their decks to see what the noise was. Porch lights clicked on. I knew a couple of cats had made it onto the wagon for a free ride. I could hear them screeching at each other. On and on I went. It felt like a carpet of cats at my feet. An ocean of fur and tails. Surely the missing cats had to be there!

When I got close to Mr. Taylor's house, I heard cheering. A crowd of kids stood on the lawn. I felt like a hero. What a victory parade! What a story! I hoped Quentin brought his camera.

In the light of Mr. Taylor's street lamp, I could see about 20 cats following the wagon. Chuckie sat in the middle of a dozen more cats. He was meowing just like they were.

The closer I came to the crowd, the better I heard the cheering. Or, what I'd thought was cheering.

It wasn't.

Instead of cheering, angry voices were calling to me. "What are you doing?" somebody hollered.

"Where's my cat?" yelled another.

All around the wagon, cats faced each other. Their backs arched. They spat. They growled.

"Who does she think she is? The Pied Piper of Cats?"

I pulled to a stop in front of the crowd. People rushed the wagon. Mrs. Bell, Haley's piano teacher, lifted her Siamese cat, Bach. Bach tried to squirm free. "Molly Mack," she said. "What will your mother say about this?"

Mr. Turner, Mrs. Baker, Jeremy, and Eric the Red (a red-haired Vulture) claimed their cats. "Are you nuts?" Eric asked, grabbing his black cat from Chuckie's lap.

The rest of the crowd moved in. They scrambled for their cats.

Mr. Taylor put his hand on my head. "I don't see Ashley's cat, Molly."

Then he looked again. "Unless ... Fluffy?" He bent down and lifted a long white-haired cat. "What's happened, boy?" he asked.

Fluffy looked fine—except for one thing. A big chunk of white fur had been cut off!

Kyle was sniffling back tears. "Big Shot's back!" he yelled. "But somebody took a bunch of her hair!"

Nicole and her mother came walking up the sidewalk. "Where's Tiger?" Nicole called.

A few cats still stirred around the wagon. One of the cats pranced out to meet Nicole. "What happened to her fur?" she asked, scooping up Tiger.

I looked at Tiger. A patch of hair was missing. Somebody had shaved a stripe down her back. It made her look like a skunk. "Weird," I said.

"I don't care," Nicole said. "I've got my Tiger back."

But Nicole was the only one who left happy. Everybody else grumbled as they grabbed their cats and checked them over.

When I thought everybody was gone except Chuckie, me, Callie, and a few unknown cats, Quentin crept out from the bushes. "Well," he said weakly. "I guess that's the end of the cat caper. The lost cats have been found."

"No way!" I said. "Now there's even more of a mystery! *Who* took cat hair from the missing cats?"

I was already starting to see tomorrow's headlines. "Cinnamon Lake won't be safe until we expose the fur-stealing cat burglar!"

7

Interesting Truth

Friday morning, the *Cinnamon Lake News* sold like hot chocolate at the North Pole. And no wonder, with headlines like these:

Hair-Stealing Cat Burglar Loose in Cinnamon Lake!

Screaming Cats Haunt Cinnamon Drive

Cinnamon Lake Mystery Club Close to Solving Mystery

Still, I had a funny feeling inside me. And I couldn't figure out why. The cats were home safe. Minus a few hairs. Quentin had refused to help with the paper. But it didn't matter. Haley helped a lot. And the Vultures hadn't even bothered to put out a Friday *VIP*.

So why was I feeling like a water-logged woodpecker? I pushed the feeling aside.

"Congratulations, Molly!" Sam said. He leaned against the paper rack and folded his arms across his chest. "I have to hand it to you."

I couldn't help blushing. Sam Benson was congratulating *me*. "Well—" I fumbled for something to say.

Sam pointed to the headline about being close to solving the mystery. "That one's my favorite," he said.

"I came up with that one all by myself," I admitted.

"Really, Molly," Sam continued. "My brother Ben said he didn't know you had it in you."

Wow! Even Ben Benson was impressed? "Ben really liked it?" I asked.

"Yeah!" Sam said. "Ben's very words to Marty were, 'Who would have thought Molly Mack could lie like a Vulture!'"

Lie? *Gulp!* "But I ... we ... didn't *lie*," I said. "We just presented the truth in a more interesting way."

"That's great!" Sam shouted. "I love it. Wait till I tell Ben and Marty. Truth in a more interesting way!" Sam ran off, still laughing.

Mr. Winkle pulled in. The bus front bumper caught the stop sign with a thump. We piled on.

I plopped down in a seat by myself. It hadn't felt like lying when we made up our headlines. We answered *when, where,* and *what.* Facts. Sam didn't know what he was talking about.

The bus stopped, and Ashley got on. I wondered how much she knew about the cat parade. And Fluffy's new hairdo.

From across the aisle, Sam yelled, "Hey, Ashley! Could I borrow Fluffy? I have a white fur coat to finish."

Ben chimed in. "What's the matter? *Cat* got your tongue?"

Ashley kept her nose in the air. Twice she turned and glared at me, like it was *my* fault.

When I stepped off the bus, Ben was already giving Kyle a hard time. "Kyle, what's purr-fectly sunk? A bald cat who's used up all nine lives!" He laughed and walked away, leaving Kyle close to tears.

"Molly," Kyle said. "I'm afraid for Big Shot. What if someone comes back for the rest of her fur? Do the Cinnamon Lakers really have inside information like you said?"

Well, we were *inside* when we wrote that article. I didn't know what to say. Truth in an interesting way?

"I'll try to get the truth for you, Kyle," I promised. "The real truth."

The real truth. My Sunday school teacher always said Jesus was the real truth—and the true way to heaven. I took a big breath. Jesus, I prayed, I'm not sure how I got in this mess. Help me know what to do.

After school, the Cinnamon Lake Mystery Club met in our tree. From my branch, I could look across the lake at the Vulture club house.

"Get on with it," Quentin grumbled. "I do not have time for this cat nonsense."

"It's not nonsense," Haley said.

"Come on, Quentin," I said. "We need you. We've got to answer the next *W. Who* stole the cats?"

"Nonsense," Quentin said. "No one stole cats."

"All right then," I said. "Who cut their fur off?"

Before Quentin could object, I brought out my notebook. "We need a list of suspects." I wrote *Who* at the top of the page. "Who do you think might have done it?"

"Sam," Haley said.

"Why?"

"Shifty eyes?" Haley answered.

"That's not a good reason," I said. But I wrote Sam Benson's name on the *Who* page. "Eric the Red spent Tuesday night with his grandmother," I said. "So he's out."

We were quiet for a minute. I thought I heard Quentin's gray cells turning.

"That leaves Marty and Ben," I said, writing it down. "Quentin, Marty is *your* cousin. Do you think he would steal cats?"

"Marty would steal our grandmother if he thought he could get a few dollars for her."

"How about Off-Her-Rocker Crocker?" Haley asked.

"Don't call her that, Haley," I said. Mrs. Crocker lives by herself deep in the woods. A lot of kids at Cinnamon are scared of her because she looks and dresses different. But she's really nice once you get to know her. "Mrs Crocker is not a suspect!"

An hour later, we still had only three names on my *Whodunit* list.

"This is it then," I said. "Ben, Sam, and Marty. We can each take a name and question the suspect. Too bad Dirt can't be in on this. She's the only one who could get the truth out of Ben Benson."

"You can be glad Dirt's not here!" Haley shouted. "She's crazier than usual these days."

"Dirt's just pouring herself into her experiment," I said. "She'll be fine."

"Experiment? Dirt?" Quentin asked.

"Dirt's trying to come up with a new color—*dirt*," I explained. "She thinks she's almost got it."

"Anyway," Haley whined. "We don't need her. *I'll* take Ben Benson."

"Yoohoo?" Quentin said in his cracked voice.

"Are you sure, Haley?" I asked. "Do you want me to go with you?"

"No, I'll be fine. You two just worry about Marty and Sam." Haley studied her nail polish. Then she gathered her flowered skirt in one hand and climbed down.

Speechless, Quentin and I stared after her.

"This does not compute," Quentin said. "Haley has always been afraid of Ben Benson."

I shook my head. "Maybe she's growing up?"

Quentin gave me his "Sure, she is" look. "Listen, Molly," he began. "About this interview. It is not necessary. I ..."

"Don't you back out on me, Quentin!" I said. "Come on! I'll even take Marty. You can have Sam."

Inside, I hoped Quentin would insist on taking his cousin. Instead, Quentin sighed. "Oh, all right."

We started for the other side of the lake, where Marty and Sam live. I led the way through the woods and back up to Cinnamon Drive. Just as we rounded the corner, an Amish buggy appeared, drawn by a bay mare. You'd think I'd be used to seeing Amish people by now. They live on farms all around us.

There is something honest about the way they all dress. Black or dark blue. Men in hats.

Women in bonnets. They seem friendly and happy, even without TV or cars or movies.

"Sometimes I wish I could be Amish," I said.

"You would not last three days without electricity," Quentin said.

We waved as their buggy horse trotted past us. That's when I saw something very strange. Quentin had scratches up and down his arm!

"Quentin, where did you get those scratches?"

Quentin jerked his sleeve down. "No-where. I don't have any scratches." He ran across the road. "I'll take the shortcut to Sam's," he yelled. And he was off before I could say another word.

I didn't move. I'd seen scratches on his arm. Why did he pretend I didn't? And where would Quentin get scratches like that? He spends most of his time in his science lab in his basement.

I didn't like the thought that was tickling my gray cells. Those scratches? Could they have been made by cats? I'd told Jesus I wanted to learn the truth. But did it have to be about Quentin?

8

Marty? Sam? Ben? Or ...?

I couldn't get Quentin's scratches out of my mind. Before I knew it, I was halfway to Marty's. I looked up, my gaze following a giant leaf. It sailed past me. Then who should I see heading right at me but Marty himself! He looked like a firecracker ready to explode!

"Marty!" I jogged to the middle of the road to meet him.

Marty is as tall and lean as his cousin Quentin is short and chubby. I was afraid Marty was going to storm by me. "What do you want, Mack?" Marty gave me a look that made me feel like I had spaghetti on my face.

"Just a couple of questions. About the cats?" I said weakly.

"What cats?" Marty asked, as if I had asked about Martians.

He bent to tie his shoelace. It gave me a chance to study him. His brown hair was shaved smooth. He wore tan slacks and a plaid, wool shirt. Then I saw that all over that shirt were little, white hairs.

I held my breath. Could those hairs be Fluffy hairs?

"Outta my way, Mack," he said, pushing me aside.

I hate being called by my last name. Marty knows it—which, of course, is why he calls me *Mack*.

He brushed past me and strode off down the middle of the road. All I knew was I couldn't let him get away. I waited until he turned the corner. Then I followed him.

I ducked behind trees. I dove into ditches filled with musty leaves. Marty turned left out of Cinnamon Lake onto County Road 620. Me too. Marty took another left. So did I.

He passed the Amish school. The small, white building sat empty. The children were probably out working the fields or milking.

Where could Marty be going, I wondered. I watched from behind a barn. There were nothing but farms and fields out that way. Except for the Animal Clinic. And ... Getz

Pets. Of course! Marty was heading for the pet store!

Getz Pets was just an old house Mr. Getz had turned into a pet store. I wished I'd made Quentin come with me. If I could catch Marty buying cat food, or selling cat hair, I'd solve the mystery!

I waited until Marty went in. Then I rushed to the window. Two cages of what looked like rats blocked my view. I'd have to go inside.

I opened the door, and a bell rang. It scared me half to death!

"May I help you?" asked a little man with a beaglelike face. Mr. Getz.

I glanced around for Marty. Puppies whined in cages along one wall. A giant snake slept behind glass. But no Marty.

"Did you see a tall, skinny customer come in a minute ago?" I asked.

Mr. Getz frowned. "*You* are my customer," he said. "My only customer at the moment. May I show you something?"

Why was he hiding Marty? I saw Marty go in! Maybe Mr. Getz was in on the cat fur business. Maybe he had some way to sell the cat hair Marty brought him!

"Hey! Did you clean them cages before you put them mice in there?" Mr. Getz's gruff shout took me by surprise. I turned to see who he was yelling at.

"Marty?" I could hardly believe my eyes!

Marty was carrying a cage full of mice! He wore a *Getz Petz* cap and big, gray gloves. "Did you follow me?" Marty barked. He scowled his eyebrows into a V. It made him look like a real vulture.

I opened my mouth, but couldn't get any words out. Marty didn't wait. He picked up a handful of white mice and set them on his shoulders. They scattered all up and down his arms and on his head. Then he dragged the empty cages to the back of the store.

"Been working here a week. Not the best worker," Mr. Getz said as we stared after Marty. "Working off a—a kind of personal debt. Still, the kid has a gift with rats and mice."

I tried not to laugh. "Rats and mice? Those *white* mice?"

"Of course," said Mr. Getz.

So that explained the white hair. Marty wouldn't have had time to steal cats anyway. I hurried out, leaving Marty to the mice.

Quentin was waiting for me when I got back. I filled him in on Marty's alibi.

"My grandmother told me Marty got caught shoplifting," Quentin said. "I knew he had to earn money to pay the store back. I didn't know it was the pet shop."

"What about Sam?" I asked.

"Sam has been grounded all week," he said.

"That leaves Ben," I said. "Wonder how Haley made out with him."

We found Haley sipping hot chocolate on her front porch.

Quentin and I sat on the step below Haley. Bright yellow leaves dropped from the oak tree above us.

"Marty and Sam aren't the cat burglars," I explained. "They both have alibis."

"Are you sure?" Haley asked.

"We're sure," I said. "What about Ben?"

Haley shook her head. "Huh uh."

"Well, that is it then," Quentin said quickly. "We do not know who did it. And I cannot see that it matters. Case closed." He started to get up.

I jerked him back down. "Wait! It has to be Ben!" I said. "He probably lied to Haley."

"It wasn't Ben," Haley said. "Ben's allergic to cats. He couldn't steal a cat. He'd be sneezing his head off."

"How do you know?" I asked.

"My mother goes to the same allergy doctor Ben goes to," Haley said. "And your mother too, Quentin."

"So," Quentin snarled. "You didn't even talk to Ben?"

"No. Why would I?" Haley whined.

"Why would you?" Quentin repeated through clenched teeth. "Why would you?" He stood and pointed his finger at Haley. When he did, the scratches on his right arm poked out of his green jacket.

"What's on your arm?" Haley asked, getting to her feet.

Quentin threw his hands behind his back. "None of your business!" he screamed.

"Stop it, you two!" I begged. "We've got a cat caper to solve here. If Ben didn't do it ... And Marty and Sam didn't do it ... Who-dunit?"

Quentin and Haley faced off against each other. Their noses were so close, they could have sneezed for each other. "Maybe Quentin did it," Haley said.

9

The Story of Oreos

Quentin's mouth dropped open.

"You heard me," Haley yelled. "Quentin hates cats! He's always doing experiments. Maybe he decided to use cats in some stupid experiments."

"I ... I ... I do not have to stay here another moment!" Quentin sputtered. "I have no time to listen to the ravings of someone who thinks Isaac Newton is a country western singer!" He stomped off.

"Don't go, Quentin!" I yelled. "Now look what you've done, Haley. Quentin is the most honest boy I know."

"A lot you know about honesty, Molly Mack the News Woman," she said. "*Screaming Cats Haunt Cinnamon Drive?* Sound familiar?"

I ran after Quentin. It gave me time to think. And pray. I had suspected Quentin too. His arms *were* scratched. In fact, ever since I'd started "telling truth in an interesting way," I didn't know who to trust. Dishonesty was like Dirt's food coloring. A little bit spread and colored everything. "Help me, Jesus," I whispered. "Help me know the truth."

When I caught up with Quentin, he was in front of his house. Instead of going inside, he walked around to his mother's prize rosebush. He was staring into the bush when I walked up.

How was I going to ask him about the scratches on his arm—without making him mad? "Quentin?" I called.

Quentin wheeled around and held his finger to his lips. Then he stared into the rosebush again.

"What are you doing?" I whispered.

Instead of answering, he reached into the thickest part of the rosebush. A few dead red roses were still hanging on, but most were gone.

I peered inside the bush and saw a package of something black. "Oreo cookies?" I cried.

"Not so loud!" Quentin said. His arms were deep in the bush now. "My mother does not approve of Oreos."

"But how did they get in your rosebush?" I asked.

"My grandmother gave me the package yesterday. I was eating cookies on the porch when Mother drove up. All I could do was toss them over the side ... and into the rosebush."

Quentin pulled his hand from the bush. In it was what was left of an Oreo cookie bag. His eyes grew as big as Oreos as he popped a cookie into his mouth.

He rubbed his arm. "Hmmm. I guess I scratched myself trying to get them."

So that was how he got his scratches! Roses! Not cats.

I was about to tell Quentin the truth about my suspicions. I wanted to go back to the old, honest way of reporting. I didn't like not trusting each other.

But just then, the front door banged open. Out charged Quentin's mother.

Quentin threw the cookies at me. I juggled them from one hand to the other. Then I threw them back under the rosebush.

"Oh, Quentin!" said his mother. "A-Ah-Ahchoo!" Her brown business suit was wrinkled. She held a man's huge handkerchief in her fist.

"Not again, Mother?" Quentin asked.

"I can't stop sneezing! I'm on my way to the allergy doctor," she cried.

As Quentin's mom sneezed her way to her car, Sam and Haley walked up. "Did you hear about Off-Her-Rocker Crocker?" Sam yelled.

I was too tired to correct Sam. "What?"

"Somebody threw rotten eggs at her house!" Sam said.

"No!" I shouted. "Why? Mrs. Crocker never bothers anybody! Why did they do it, Sam?"

"They sprayed shaving cream on her window," Sam said. "It spelled out: GO AWAY, CAT BURGLAR!"

"But she didn't do anything!" I said.

"Maybe not," Sam said. "But your article got everybody kind of crazy. Somebody was bound to blame Crocker."

I wanted to drag myself off, throw a blanket over my head, and hide. My "interesting" headlines had done this to Mrs. Crocker. I let out a low groan.

Callie Cat must have heard me. She came running toward us. Sam picked her up. "Hey!" he yelled. "Look!" Sam pointed to a small spot behind Callie's ear. A teaspoon of hair had been cut off! "The mad cat cutter strikes again!" Sam said.

Haley leaned in to examine the cut. "I think it looks like the letter *C*," she said. "Maybe it's a secret message from the cat burglar."

"Nonsense!" Quentin grumbled. "You can hardly tell any hair is missing."

"Well," Sam said, setting Callie down. "Don't steal our headline."

Headlines. I didn't care if we ever printed another *Cinnamon Lake News.* I couldn't stop thinking about Mrs. Crocker. If I hadn't scared people with my "interesting" headlines ... . "As soon as we solve this mystery," I said, "the Cinnamon Lakers are getting out of the newspaper business."

"Why?" Haley whined.

"Yeah, why?" Sam asked.

Why! Of course! That was it! We'd worked on who, what, when, where ... but *Why?* I'd forgotten all about Quentin's most important *W! Why* would someone need cat fur?

"Yuk! Get that dirty cat away from me!" Haley's scream broke my thoughts. Callie had rubbed against her, muddying Haley's tights. "Look what that cat did!" she whined. "Now I'm all dirty!"

Dirty? *Dirty* cat? A light in my gray cells tried to click on. *Dirty?* Could that explain *why?* "Quentin!" I yelled. "You were right all along! It all comes down to *why!*"

"Molly, I do not doubt that I was correct all along. Yet I do not understand your point."

"Come with me, everybody!" I said. "I think I just figured out *why* someone needed cat fur!"

10

Why, Oh, Why?

I led the race to Dirt's. "Just give me a few minutes," I begged. "I think we can get to the bottom of this mystery."

Mrs. Harrison met us in the front hall. She looked like she had gained weight overnight. She was eating chocolate chip cookie dough ice cream out of a gallon container. When she saw us, she hid it behind her back.

"Oh, hello," she said, wiping ice cream from her fake smile. "Haley, why are these children here?"

Haley shrugged.

"We need to see Dirt," I said.

"Well, I think that might be all right. She is nearly well." Mrs. Harrison waved us on upstairs, while she backed out of the room.

"Molly," Quentin said as we ran up the stairs. "I demand to know what this is all about!"

We were in front of Dirt's bedroom door. I knocked.

"Enter!" came Dirt's voice from inside.

We entered. There sat Dirt, holding an ugly, grayish cat. A stuffed cat!

"What do you think?" she said proudly. "It's *dirt* colored!"

"Pouffy!" Haley screeched. "You've ruined her!" Haley grabbed Dirt's prize out of her hands.

"Cool, huh?" Dirt said.

"I know why you took the *real* cats, Dirt," I said. I waded across her room and sat beside her. "You cut off their hair because you wanted to try out your new color on fur. I blame myself, Dirt. If I hadn't started being dishonest, none of this would have happened."

"My own sister? A cat burglar!" Haley cried.

"How did you pull it off, Dirt?" Sam asked. His voice was full of admiration.

"Are you guys crazy?" Dirt asked. She was staring at us. "I only used stuffed animals—like Pouffy."

"I know you didn't think of it as stealing, Dirt," I said. "But we all have to tell the truth." I tried to go on. "Haley and I made up those headlines. Those weren't honest. You took the cats and cut off their fur for your color experiments. That wasn't honest either. Quentin is the only one who stayed honest. He—"

"Stop it!" Quentin's scream shocked me into silence. "I can't take it anymore! Dirt did not take the cats! *I* did it. I'm the one. I took the cats. I cut their fur."

"No way," Sam said.

Quentin raised his sleeve. "I have the scratches to prove it!"

"Those are from the Oreos in the bushes," I said.

"Yet another clever story to throw you off the track. Fluffy scratched me when I took a piece of her fur. I knew you suspected me because of the scratches. So I planted the cookies in the bushes. All I had to do was wait for you to come along and see me."

I couldn't believe it. *Quentin!*

"Why'd you do it, Quentin?" Sam asked.

"He did it for his experiments," Haley said. "Just like I said!"

"No!" Quentin shouted. "I did not do it for the sake of science." He took off his glasses, then put them on again. "I want a cat," he mumbled. He said it so low, I wasn't sure I heard him right.

"What did you say?" I asked.

"I want a cat!" he said louder.

"I know you're a genius and all," Sam said. "But aren't there easier ways of going about getting a cat?"

"Not if your mother believes she is allergic to cats," he said.

I remembered how his mother had sneezed and run to the allergy doctor.

Quentin continued. "I decided to try out different cats to find one Mother could live with. I thought there surely must exist one type of cat that would not make her sneeze.

"First, I tried sneaking Fluffy into the house. I hid her in my room. Mother couldn't figure out why her allergies were acting up. So I borrowed Big Shot. Different breed. Shorter hair. But Mother almost found them both. So I clipped some of their fur and turned them loose. Then I sprinkled the hairs around Mother's bedroom. She sneezed.

"That's when I took a sample of Tiger's fur. And a tiny bit from behind Callie's ear. So little, you didn't even notice when you came over last night, Molly."

Last night! "But the cat parade?" I stammered. "The cats weren't in your room then, Quentin!"

"Nor had they been for quite some time," he explained. "I had given them fish and catnip to lure them to my room. They did not wish to leave! They kept to the woods behind our yard and waited for more fish treats. I was going to use the fish and catnip to lead the cats back to their homes."

"Your bag of catnip and fish!" I said, the picture becoming clearer now.

"Indeed," Quentin said. "I had to think rather quickly to come up with a story when you and Chuckie showed up at my house."

When I thought about it, it did seem odd that Quentin just happened to be planning a parade when I walked up. He *had* hemmed and hawed when I'd asked him about his bag.

"I am very sorry," he said.

"Far out!" Dirt said.

"Wait 'til Ben hears this!" Sam said. "I gotta go! The Vultures have a paper to get out."

Sam left. Quentin, Dirt, Haley, and I apologized to each other and to our parents. And to the cat owners. We cleaned eggs and shaving cream off Mrs. Crocker's house.

Then we went to work. We had a newspaper to get out too. But no more "truth in an interesting way." This newspaper would be the truth. The *honest* truth.

Next morning, Quentin, Haley, Dirt, and I walked up to check on our papers. I wasn't surprised to see most of ours still in the box.

We'd written the honest story of the disappearing cats. We answered *who, what, where, when,* and *why.* Mr. Adams would have been proud. More important, I knew Jesus had helped me do the right thing. The answers wouldn't make us rich. But they were honest. And that felt pretty good.

Ashley's dad drove up. He greeted us. Then he bought the last copy of the *VIP.* I read the headlines as he walked off.

Mad Scientist Experiments on Cats!
No Hair Is Safe in Cinnamon Lake!

I had to laugh. Vultures! A cold wind blew out of the north. Quentin, Haley, Dirt, and I stood in a pack to get warm.

"Cheer up, guys," I pleaded. "All the cats are home safe. Dirt's over the chicken pox. She even invented a new color. You have to admit, it feels better to be honest. Doesn't it?"

Haley rolled her eyes. "You're not going to say something corny like 'Honesty is the best policy,' are you?"

I was, but I decided not to.

Sam came running up. His hands were full of quarters from selling the *VIP*. "This is the Vultures' biggest sale ever!" he said.

Sam glanced at our unsold stack of papers. "Haven't you guys sold any?"

"Nope," I admitted.

"Too bad," Sam said.

I looked from Quentin to Haley to Dirt. "It's not so bad. *Honest!*"

Help the Cinnamon Lakers solve these mysteries too!

56-1812

56-1813

56-1833